Disney · PIXAR

TOY TEAM

A GOLDEN BOOK • NEW YORK

ISBN: 978-0-7364-2852-1
www.randomhouse.com/kids
MANUFACTURED IN CHINA
10 9 8 7 6 5 4 3 2 1
3-D special effects by Red Bird Press. All rights reserved.

Woody and Andy make a great team.

Buzz Lightyear to the rescue!

Oh, no! Woody has to help Buzz.

Woody and Buzz are one great toy team!

Woody finds his friends a ride home.

Buzz, Woody, and Jessie know they will
be okay as long as they are together.

The Aliens spot a claw!

Lotso, Twitch, Chunk, and Sparks are one tough gang!

The toys take a scary tumble together.

Woody, Hamm, and Rex tiptoe past Big Baby.

Woody and Slinky work together.

Rex and Bullseye are always glad to see Woody.

Jessie helps her friends get ready for a move.

Andy loves his toys.

These toys make a terrific team!

Woody, Buzz, and Bullseye work together to save Jessie.

Rex gives Hamm and Slinky a boost.

Buzz and Slinky team up to help Woody.

The Prospector traps the Roundup gang!

The toys are on a mission!

Buzz finds—himself!

Hamm and Rex cruise the aisles of Al's Toy Barn together.

Buzz is a brave leader.

Woody is thrilled to learn he's part of Woody's Roundup!

Buzz rushes to Woody's rescue.

Woody helps a friend—and gets stuck at a yard sale!

Buzz lends Woody a helping hand.

Buzz and Woody make a quick escape.

Buzz and Woody shake on a job well done.

Woody and the mutant toys work together to scare Sid.

Woody gives Buzz a pep talk.